SACRIFICE FOR LOVE

AMISH ROMANCE

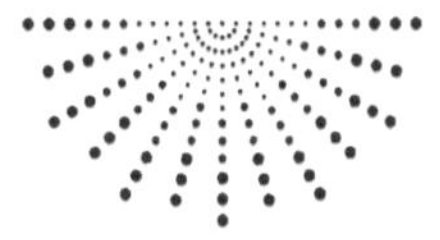

SARAH MILLER

JOIN MY NEWSLETTER

UNTITLED

https://www.createapeacefulhome.com/scripture-exercises/15-bible-verses-help-de-stress/

next psalm 94:

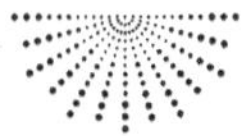

When anxiety was great within me,
your consolation brought me joy.
Psalm 94:19

Anna Sutter had a good life, all things considered. *Gott* had graced her with a loving *mamm* and *daed,* and a younger *schweschder* who seemed to shine as brightly as the sun.

When there were so many people in the world who had not even one person to care for them, she knew that she was blessed beyond measure. That was what made her pervasive sadness all the more difficult to bear.

She lived in an Amish community called Faith's Creek, along with the rest of her *familye*. It was the place she had been born, as had her parents before her. She had *nee* doubt at all that it would be where she lived still when it was finally time for her to go to be with *Gott*.

She thought it was probably one of the loveliest places in all of the world, although she had nothing to compare it to, and she was happy enough to stay there for the whole of her life. It wasn't where she was that made her unhappy, it was who she was inside, and she thought that must be a good deal worse.

She was a slight young woman, slender trending on the side of frail. Her deep chestnut hair was always up under the covering of her *kapp*. She was careful never to let a single strand stray out of place if she could help it. She did not like the idea of giving people a reason for her to be seen.

Her eyes were wide and almost as dark as her hair, and her skin was as pale as a fresh container of cream. Against the dark hues of the blue dresses that were her daily uniform, she worried that the extremity of her fairness made her stand out like a white sheet fluttering across a night-darkened sky. The thought alone made her tremble with dread, and it made her more than a little weary to venture outdoors more than was strictly necessary.

Perhaps worst of the long list of things she believed weren't quite right about her, was the fact that at twenty-years-old, she remained unwed. Not only was she still unmarried, when many of her peers had already begun their own happy *familye's*, but she also had nary a prospect or hope of being courted anytime soon. It seemed to her that, aside from her always loving parents and *schweschder*, nobody in Faith's Creek wanted her or would really care if she were suddenly gone.

"Such a foolish way to think," she chastised herself as she tugged mercilessly at her needle and thread. "Such a waste of energy. What does it matter if you're wanted by others at all? You contribute. You work as hard as you can to help make this *haus* a home."

She nodded to herself, glancing down at the ever-growing pile of completed mending beside her for reassuring proof. It was true that she was a hard worker, and one who never complained, and she knew her parents appreciated that about her.

Unfortunately, it was also true that if she were never able to find a man who wanted to take her for his *fraa*, she would undoubtedly prove to be a burden as her parents moved into their golden years of age. They would have to continue to care for her long past the point when parents were meant to be relieved of that task. The mere thought of it was enough to make her shudder, and her eyes well up with tears.

"*Ach*, here you are!" Anna's *schweschder*, Ruth, exclaimed from the open screen door of the back porch. "I've been looking for you all over. I thought you had gone and disappeared."

"*Nee*, I've been right here the whole time," Anna protested, her heart hammering in her chest as she tried in vain to recover from her start. "And you frightened me half to death. You shouldn't sneak up on people like that, Ruth. You really shouldn't."

"I know," Ruth said with a dramatic sigh that wasn't quite able to make up for the glint of mischief shining in her cornflower eyes. "But sometimes, I just can't seem to help myself. And, anyway, I really was looking for you, and for what felt like the longest time. Have you been out here all day?"

"Why, I don't know," Anna answered with a small frown of confusion.

She looked out from beneath the porch's comfortably weathered ceiling and gazed up at the sky, trying to determine what time it was. Truth be told, she didn't have the first clue how long she had been out there on her own. That was one of the hazards of being a person who spent most of her waking hours on her own. Time had a way of losing itself, and sometimes, of disappearing altogether.

"Well, I think you have been," Ruth said decisively, her hands on her hips as she surveyed Anna's day's work with a scrutinizing eye. "And I think it's enough for today. It's time to put your work away, too."

"*Ach*, really?" Anna asked, laughing despite herself. "And what brought you to that conclusion?"

"My keen powers of observation," Ruth said, her expression kept serious for only a moment before she collapsed into a fit of giggles that Anna couldn't help but join in.

And that was the thing about Ruth, the thing that everybody who met her couldn't help but notice. Ruth was the sort of girl that people just wanted to be around, even if they couldn't quite put their finger on why. She was funny and kind, silly, and a little bit wild, and all of those things were absolutely contagious.

In short, Anna believed that her sweet, sixteen-year-old *schweschder* was all of the things that she herself was not. Whereas Anna was likely to blend seamlessly into the background of any gathering she was forced to attend, Ruth was always like a bright, shining star in a crowd.

Everyone wanted to be around her, and although she was still just a little bit too young to begin a courtship, it was already widely understood who she would eventually marry. It was understood with a confidence that Anna couldn't remember ever having about anything in her life.

Ruth and a boy named Jonathan Knepp had been thick as thieves for as long as anyone could remember, and their friendship seemed to be naturally evolving into something far deeper. While Jonathan was about to leave for his *Rumspringa,* people expected that when he returned to Faith's Creek, he and Ruth would begin courting. They would be wed, and Anna would officially be surpassed by her lovely younger *schweschder.*

"I'm serious, Anna," she whined now, reaching for Anna's hand and trying to tug her onto her feet. "It's time to put this away. Don't you want to have a little bit of adventure in your life?"

"What?" Anna asked with surprise and not a little bit of dread. "*Nee,* of course not. What are you going on about, anyhow?"

"Nothing," Ruth answered, a pretty pout on her pert, sixteen-year-old lips. "I'm just saying that it might not be such a bad thing for you to do something other than work and shut yourself away in the *haus.*"

"It's a *wunderbaar haus,*" Anna snapped back, her tone more severe than she intended, although she didn't seem to make it otherwise. "And I don't mind the work. I'm happy to do it. I'm happy to be useful to our parents. I think they need me to do what I do, anyhow. What would they think if I just ran off?"

"They would be pleased for you to have a little time to yourself," Ruth answered immediately, and with a confidence that Anna didn't think she had ever felt before in her life. "I was talking to *Mamm*…"

"About me?" Anna interrupted, finally getting to her feet as Ruth had wanted her to all along. "The two of you were talking about me without me being there?"

"*Jah,* but not anything bad," Ruth insisted, finally showing the faintest hint of uncertainty. "I was telling her that I wished the two of us spent more time together. Time outside of the *haus,* and she said she thought that was a lovely idea. She is the one who bade me come and find you. She told me you should come with me to game night."

That stopped Anna cold. The idea that two of the people she loved most in the world had come together to speak about the extent to which she was isolating herself made her feel exposed and ashamed.

It was the very feeling she feared most, and so she kept herself apart as if it might keep her safe.

And yet, at the same time, there was a part of her that saw what Ruth was saying now as an opportunity. She saw it as a chance being offered to her, one that she was sorely tempted to take. Perhaps she wasn't destined to live out her days alone, after all, as unlikely as the possibility seemed. Maybe forcing herself to come out of her shell a little would offer her one of *Gott's* many blessings and rewards.

"*Jah*," she said softly before she had time to convince herself not to speak at all.

"What?" Ruth asked, her eyes growing wide with disbelief. "What did you say?"

"I said *Jah*," Anna repeated, smiling at her *schweschder's* obvious delight despite the butterflies fluttering wildly in her stomach. "All right. I'll accompany you into town tonight, just so long as you promise not to try and turn it into a habit."

Instead of answering, Ruth threw her arms around Anna's neck. Anna understood that Ruth's failure to agree to her terms meant that there would likely be similar requests in the future. At the moment, however, she found that she didn't really care. She was going to allow herself an adventure, and despite it being a small one, she was excited for what may come to pass.

but those who hope in the Lord
will renew their strength.
They will soar on wings like eagles;
they will run and not grow weary,
they will walk and not be faint.
Isaiah 40:31

Anna's happy feelings about agreeing to accompany Ruth into town lasted for as long as it took to reach the outskirts. As soon as she saw the first buildings that marked what passed as Faith's Creek's little Main Street, however, her doubts came flooding back, and with full force.

What on earth had she been thinking, to agree to come with Ruth, not just here, but anywhere at all? Ruth was like the sun, while she, Anna, was like a deep night sky without the benefit of stars. Who could possibly want to have that kind of darkness in their lives when the brightness of the day was willing to shine down upon them?

"Please, Anna, stop," Ruth scolded gently, holding onto Anna's hand and tugging her gently forward when the older girl's steps began to falter. "The evening's festivities haven't even begun yet. Won't you try not to convince yourself that it will all be a disaster before you even give it a try?"

"Of course," Anna answered automatically, although her voice sounded wooden to her own ears. "Nobody said I was thinking that way."

Except that she was, of course. It was exactly what she was thinking, and Ruth knew her too well for her to hide it completely. At the moment, Anna was too nervous even to try and hide it. She was on the verge of panic, a feeling that hailed completely from the knowledge that she was very soon going to be at the mercy of people she did not trust to treat her with kindness.

For some reason, Anna had simply never learned how to interact with parts of the world around her as her peers had done. This was especially true when it came to any sort of dealings with the opposite sex. Many of the other girls had been friends with boys when Anna was growing up, but she had never been able to more than glance at them for a moment, and that for only a moment.

"Come on," Ruth said confidently, ignoring what Anna was sure must be obvious signs of her distress. "The barn is just a little further up the road, and the games are going to be so much fun! You'll get used to being there and with the others in *nee* time at all. I have *nee* doubt!"

Anna nodded, although she was sure that she was full of enough doubts for the both of them. She was allowing herself to be led into a gathering of people who were all her *schweschder's* friends, even the ones who were closer to Anna's own age.

Ruth was far too sweet and hopeful to believe that this might be a problem, but Anna understood that she could never be as popular as Ruth was. Anna wasn't the sort of girl that people wanted at their gatherings, let alone the kind of guest they would be interested in talking to.

"*Ach,* here you are!" Came a chorus of greetings before Ruth had even gotten the door to the barn all of the way open. "We thought you would never come!"

"Of course I've come," Ruth said with a delighted laugh, glancing quickly over her shoulder and giving Anna a reassuring nod. "And it's even better than that. I've brought somebody along with me for a change."

With this proclamation, Ruth stepped aside, taking away Anna's last remaining bit of cover. It left her utterly exposed, clinging desperately to the edges of her apron and wishing with all of her might that she might spontaneously disappear.

Except that she did not vanish, instead, she remained very much in view and a strong point of curiosity for everyone present for the games. She thought it very likely that everyone would have gone right on staring at her, completely unabashedly, if Ruth hadn't animated and captured their collective attention.

"Well now, let's see, now that we're all here, it seems we can begin," Ruth said brightly, clapping her hands with unadulterated delight. "And of course we must all catch up with one another. I want to hear everything new that's happened to anyone."

"But, Ruth," a girl named Faith chirped brightly, her face showing cheerful, all-encompassing admiration. "We've all seen each other only a few days ago."

"True, but even so, life has a way of happening quickly, don't you think?" Ruth countered with a smile, a shrug, and a little twinkle in her eye that made everyone around her chuckle.

Ruth hurried forward into the crowd of young people, all of whom she could surely count as a friend. She looked at Anna over her shoulder as she went, and the expression on her face was clear. It was a pleading look, one that beseeched Anna to set aside her idiosyncrasies just for once so that she might join in the fun and fellowship.

Not for the first time, Anna realized that despite

being the elder of the two *schweschders,* she felt very much like the *kinner* to Ruth's adult. It didn't seem to matter whether or not she wanted to join in with the happy conversations surrounding her. She simply wasn't able to do so.

Every step she took felt as though she were walking over a thick coating of molasses, and even the thought of opening her mouth to speak made her sick to her stomach. For the life of her, she couldn't understand how the others could do it.

She couldn't figure out how others could get along with people so effortlessly, while she remained so much on her own, *nee* matter how many people she was with. The only place she felt at ease was with her parents, back in their lovely little farm *haus,* and she longed to go back there now.

If she hadn't worried about letting Ruth down, and of remaining a spinster and thus placing a burden on her parents' shoulders, she would have turned right around and fled. As it was, she stood rooted to the floor, feeling very much like a fish out of water who was struggling to breathe.

"Anna, come and join us," Ruth called merrily, gesturing with one hand for Anna to join in a conversation between her and a boy named Amos. "Amos is just telling me the funniest story about some trouble he got into with one of the cows on his *familye* farm."

Anna nodded and did her best to smile, although she was sure that everyone in the barn must be able to see the way her mouth was trembling. When everything about her was shaking so badly, how in the world was she supposed to speak or laugh with anyone?

It was all she could think about, what a failure she would be at the whole thing *nee* matter what she tried, and it caused her to bow her head and look at the floor instead of the people trying to talk to her. It put them off, and she could see it, but she didn't know how to change.

"Anna, please," Ruth said, pulling her aside where the others couldn't hear and looking at her with concern. "There's really *nee* need to be so on edge. Don't you think you might loosen up a little? Just a bit?"

"Of course, sweet *schweschder*," Anna answered at once, despite having *nee* confidence in being able to do what she was asking. "It shouldn't be that hard, should it?"

"*Nee,* not at all!" Ruth said happily, the look of relief on her pretty face unmistakable. "That's exactly what I've been trying to tell you all along."

And Anna did try, she really did, and she kept Ruth's words in her head constantly. She told herself that there was *nee* reason to be nervous and that her words surely couldn't sound to the others as bungled as they felt in her head. She told herself these things in the hopes that she might truly be able to have an adventure of her own, and with the desire to please Ruth.

Still, when Ruth's attention was called away by Jonathan, Anna couldn't stop the spike of fear that cut through her belly and straight into her heart. She didn't want Ruth to walk off and leave her on her own. It would only serve to make it more painfully evident that she had *nee* true friends of her own at the gathering.

"Stop it," she whispered to herself fiercely, doing her best to adopt an outward confidence that she didn't actually feel. "This is only more of the same foolishness Ruth has been speaking to you about. These things will never get any better if you don't put yourself out there and try."

She nodded briefly, rolling her shoulders back and lifting her chin in her best imitation of confidence. As inadequate as she might feel, she was still the elder of the Sutter *schweschders* by a good four years. She was more than capable of approaching one of the nearby clusters of chatting people and joining in their conversation.

"I feel sorry for her, really," she heard one of the young men say, a sentiment that was accompanied by low murmurs and a not-so-friendly chuckle. "To have things be that way."

"Feel bad for which one of them?" Another person said, which led to another bout of giggles that made Anna's heart stop in her chest.

"For both of them," was the answer, which was exactly what Anne knew would be said.

With a hand pressed to her mouth, she turned swiftly, walking away from the group she had just been preparing to join. She only just managed to hurl herself outside of the barn's doors before her tears began to fall.

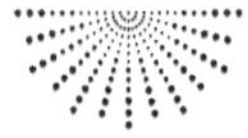

CHAPTER THREE

⁷But we have this treasure in jars of clay to show that this all-surpassing power is from God and not from us.
⁸We are hard pressed on every side, but not crushed; perplexed, but not in despair;
⁹persecuted, but not abandoned; struck down, but not destroyed.
2 Corinthians 4:7-9

Once outside of the barn and away from the stinging conversation of those who found her ridiculous, Anna lost track of time. Her grief and shame were so consuming that the world might have stopped spinning while she stood in the steadily deepening twilight, and she would never have even noticed.

Those mocking judgments shouldn't have come as a surprise, and yet to Anna, they absolutely had. It was that shock that stung the worst of all. It was the fact that she had allowed herself to believe, if only for a moment, that she might be able to get along with the world as effortlessly as sweet Ruth did.

"Stupid," she muttered to herself in a voice far harsher than any she would ever use with another person. "How could you have been so awfully stupid?"

She buried her face in her hands and succumbed to a fresh wave of tears. Before coming to this gathering, she had believed she had used up her lifelong allotment of tears in its entirety. Now, she was humbled to realize just how wrong she had been.

When she was reasonably sure that her tears were

coming to an end, and that Ruth wasn't going to come outside after her, Anna resolved that it was time for her to return home.

Once she got up the courage to pull her hands away from her face, knowing that it would be tear-streaked and awful, she would put one foot in front of the other until she was back inside of the *haus'* warm embrace. And once she was back at home with the parents who would never laugh at her shyness? Why she might never venture back out into the world again.

"Excuse me, miss," a low, warm voice said, seemingly from someplace in thin air. "I'm sorry to interrupt, but I thought you might have a use for this."

"*Ach!*" Anna gasped, her head snapping up, and her eyes feeling far too wide above her covered mouth. "You startled me. I... I didn't see you there. I'm sorry, I must look a terrible fright, carrying on this way."

"*Nee,* please," the voice said again as its owner stepped out of the shadows and beneath one of the lanterns hung above the door of the barn. "There's *nee* need for you to apologize. Especially when I'm the one who frightened you. Forgive me, please."

Anna offered her unexpected companion a smile that she hoped looked brave, but thought likely looked merely tremulous instead. Once outside of the barn doors, she had expected to find herself completely alone. It made the appearance of this stranger all the more jarring.

Except that, as the shock of his being there at all wore off, she realized that he wasn't a stranger at all. Of course, he wasn't. One wasn't likely to come across a stranger in Faith's Creek. The man before her, a hand clutching a handkerchief still extended in front of him, was Caleb Hartzler.

Caleb was one of Faith's Creek's farmers, he was a little older than Anna was herself. She had *nee* personal experience with him. However, she knew him a little by reputation. From what she understood, he was a calm, gentle man, although a quiet one, and somebody who was kind to animals.

She supposed that might be why he was so gentle with her now. Perhaps, in her current miserable state, she seemed to him akin to a wounded animal. She wasn't sure how to feel about the idea, but it also didn't stop her from gratefully accepting the handkerchief he was offering her.

"What are you doing here, anyway?" he asked now, cocking his head a little to the side and regarding her with frank, if still kind curiosity. "Were you playing the games?"

"I... *jah*," she answered weakly, although it felt too close to a lie for comfort. "I suppose you might say that. And what about you? I never even saw you inside, so you couldn't have been playing."

"*Nee, nee* games for me, I'm afraid," he chuckled, a surprisingly warm sound that made Anna shiver despite the warmth of the evening breeze. "I'm here to act as a chaperone to the festivities. My job is to see that nobody gets into too much trouble."

"Well, it looks like you're doing it well," Anna said, flushing as she spoke.

In truth, she had *nee* idea if he was doing his job or not. She would have to be a part of the fun and games for that, and she was on the outside. Just like she had been for so much of her life, she was on the outside and trying not to look in.

"You know, as a chaperone, part of what concerns me is that everyone has a good time playing the games," Caleb continued, the look of concern deepening in his eyes. "And, if you'll pardon my saying, you don't look like you're enjoying yourself."

"*Nee*," Anna said before she could stop herself, then she shook her head, more flustered now than ever. "I mean, I'm having a perfectly fine time. I think it's just time for me to go home."

"Did you play any games?" he continued, following her a couple of steps with his question as she started away on unsteady feet. "What did you play?"

"I didn't play anything," she said, her voice taking on the wooden sound that it always got when she was so nervous she could hardly get her mouth open to speak. "I... I never got around to it."

"Well, perhaps you and I could play a board game, then," he said, his tone rich and sure as it was mild. "I know it might not seem like the most fun, playing with the chaperone, but it's been a long while since I've sat down to play anything, and I think I'd like the opportunity. What do you say?"

Anna stopped, then turned to face him, truly flummoxed by what she was hearing. She couldn't recall the last time somebody had requested her company for anything. She suspected that was because nobody ever had, at least not truly.

There was a part of her that wanted to accept his invitation. The temptation was strong enough that she was caught off guard. She might have given into it and told him *jah,* too, if it hadn't been for the people still gathered inside of the barn.

Their reactions to her had ranged from something that felt a lot like scorn to pity. She wasn't sure which one was worse, but she knew that taking Caleb up on his offer would only make matters worse.

"*Denke* for the offer, really," she said, her hands clasped tightly in front of her and her eyes downcast. "But I think I must decline. I'm suddenly feeling very tired, and I think I had better go home."

"It's a wise decision," he said with a grin that made Anna decide on the spot that she liked him. "I won't lie to you; I can be a little long in the tooth sometimes. Not something that improves the quality of gameplay."

"*Nee,*" she laughed, surprised at how good it felt to do so. "I don't think that's true at all."

"Well, whether it is or not, I completely understand your desire to get home," Caleb said with a twinkle in his eye. "But I'd also like to ask if you will allow me to walk you there. I would feel better if you would let me do that."

She ought to say *nee*. She knew that, or at the very least, suspected it to be true. A walk alone with the chaperone was just as likely to invite ridicule as a board game would. Even so, she was so relieved to have somebody finally seem to see her, and to care about what she wanted, that she found herself nodding *jah* before she was even sure what she was doing.

She was so relieved to be leaving the party when they started down the road that she felt a kind of buoyancy she couldn't recall experiencing since early childhood.

She told herself that it was that happiness that made her keep glancing in Caleb's direction as they walked. She assured herself that her discreet looks at his face were born out of gratitude, and definitely not from the handsomeness of that face.

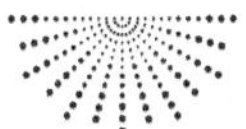

CHAPTER FOUR

Cast your cares on the LORD
and he will sustain you;
he will never let
the righteous be shaken.
Psalm 52:22

Anna and Caleb walked in silence for a little while, the seconds stretched into minutes with each new footfall. As they moved, Anna's mind began to race, full of worry that her agreeing to let Caleb walk her home had been a mistake.

She was terrified that it would only further solidify in her the knowledge that she would never be able to be with other people. This innocent walk would prove to her that she was never going to be any good at communing with another.

There was something about Caleb, though, that settled her nerves without him even having to try. Her anxiety rattled around inside of her head as it was want to do, and then as if by some miracle, slowly retreated again. She felt calm, some of her initial happiness returning, and it allowed her to remember a little more of what she knew about her current walking companion.

"I'm not sure if this is appropriate to say," she ventured, the words finally breaking their silence and sounding completely wrong in her ears. "I'm sorry, I shouldn't say anything at all."

"*Nee,* don't apologize," he said with a warm smile that she caught only with her peripheral vision. "I don't think there's anything you could say that would warrant an apology before it's even been spoken."

"It's just... I just remembered that your *fraa* went to be with *Gott* about a year ago," she said, stumbling over her words and sure she was making an awful mess of expressing her sympathies. "I didn't know you then, I don't really know you now, but I wanted to tell you how sorry I am. I can't imagine what you've gone through."

Caleb's steps faltered for a second, nothing more than a hiccup before he regained his easy stride. It was hardly anything at all, really, but it was enough to make Anna sure that her words had been a terrible mistake. It was just more proof of how awful she was with people.

"*Denke*, Anna," he finally said, his words so soft that they were almost carried off on the evening breeze. "Truly, *denke*. It's been a while since anyone has brought Esther up in my presence. It does me good to know that people still remember her from time to time."

"I would imagine that it feels very lonely," Anna said quietly, her throat suddenly thick with feeling as she considered Caleb's loss, which was greater than anything she had ever known. "To have somebody you love so much go to be with *Gott*."

"It hasn't been easy," he agreed, his words contemplative but still, somehow, striking Anna as peaceful. "Esther has been gone for nearly a year now, and sometimes I still forget that she's gone. I'll wake up in the morning with something in my head to tell her, and then remember that she's not there."

"And did the two of you have any *kinner?*" Anna asked timidly, unsure of whether or not she should ask for those kinds of details.

This felt like new territory for her, to be sure. She had spent most of the years of her young life trying to keep from getting closer to the people around her. Now, she was opening herself up to a man she hardly even knew. She was not only inviting him to confide in her; she was hoping that he might do so.

"*Nee, nee kinner,*" he said with a sigh that made her look at his face again, and this time more closely. "That's the part that I had the hardest time with, especially at the start."

"What do you mean?" she asked before she took the time to consider if posing the question might be pressing him too far. "Or please, you don't have to answer that if you don't want to. You don't have to answer anything I ask, in fact."

"I don't mind your questions, Anna," Caleb responded warmly, and the sound of her name coming out of his mouth sent a pleasant little shiver up the length of her spine. "It's nice to talk to somebody who wants to know something about me. I'm not sure that really happens the way it should these days. Do you find that to be true?"

"*Ach,* I don't know," she answered falteringly, hugging her arms around herself tightly. It felt very much like he was peering straight into her soul, and she had never had anyone do that to her before. "I don't really have much experience with people, truth be told."

"That's all right," he said, smiling a smile that she could actually hear as he spoke. "And you're doing just fine, for what it's worth."

"*Denke,*" she said with a nervous giggle, relishing the way his words emboldened her to continue the conversation despite her uncertain footing. "And I think you might be right, now that I think about it. People don't really get to know each other, do they?"

He nodded his head, and the two of them lapsed into another bout of silence. There was something different about this one than the one at the start of their walk, though, and she wondered if this was what other people felt when they formed close friendships, and maybe even more.

Stop it, she silently chided herself, her face burning at the idea that Caleb might look at her and be able to see the thoughts racing through her mind. *You're almost home, and then the two of you will go your separate ways. So just stop your silly dreaming, and keep quiet.*

"It's the loneliness that was the hardest thing about it," he spoke up again, startling her out of her own thoughts and centering all of her attention back on him. "It would have been terribly sad to have *kinner* lose their *mamm,* but there would have been something left of the two of us, something to go on after we were both gone. Because we had *nee kinner,* my grieving was done largely in solitude. I don't think that's something anyone should do."

Despite having a tender soul, this was something that surprised Anna to hear. She had spent so much of her time feeling like an outsider that she hadn't thought enough about the support system she had.

Her parents had always been *wunderbaar* and were responsible for none of the pressure Anna felt on their behalf. Ruth, despite being different from Anna in every conceivable way, was also a loving and caring friend. In many ways, Anna was actually a very lucky young woman, indeed.

"I can only imagine," she said softly, her brow furrowed as she thought of Caleb's solitary grief. "I've never experienced anything close to your loss, but I had an aunt that went to be with *Gott*. I loved her dearly, and it was difficult when she went. Leaning on my *familye* was such an essential thing for me then."

"And you were fortunate to have them," Caleb said gravely, coming to a stop as they reached the fence surrounding her *familye haus*. "Having people that love you close by is the most precious thing in the world. And, now, it looks like I have delivered you safely to your home. This is it, is it not?"

"*Jah*," she agreed, nodding vigorously before her hands moved quickly to her *kapp* to ensure that it had not come askew. "It is. *Denke*, Caleb, for taking the time to see me home. It was very kind, and something you certainly didn't have to do."

"I enjoyed our time together," Caleb said earnestly, his clasped hands striking Anna as oddly formal and endearing. "And I feel like I should be the one to say *denke* for the company. I'm sorry that the game night wasn't more to your liking. That kind of gathering can be hard at times. With so many people crowded into one place, it can be difficult not to feel like you're entirely alone."

"I'm not sorry," Anna said, distantly shocked at the boldness of what she was saying. "It's true that I didn't enjoy the game night, but I don't regret the chance to get to know you a little better."

"As did I, Miss Sutter," he said with a smile, tipping his hat to her before taking a couple of steps backward. "I hope the rest of your evening is better than the start of it."

Anna smiled, but before she could think of anything else to say, he turned around and started back down the road, the two of them had just traversed. Her heart stuttered and then moved into her throat when she saw that.

Anna couldn't recall ever having disliked anything so much as she did watching Caleb walking away. She couldn't make any sense of it, not heads nor tails. In almost every situation, the only thing she felt when she saw somebody leaving her was relief. She was so surprised to feel the exact opposite now that she didn't even think about what she did next.

"Caleb, wait a moment, won't you?" she called out, her heart hammering so wildly that she felt like she might choke on it as she hurried from the gate to meet him again.

"Well, of course, I will," he said, turning with a mildly confused smile. "But is something the matter?"

"*Nee,*" Anna stammered, all of her typical shyness coming back to her ten-fold. "I was just wondering... I was wondering if we might be able to speak again sometime. If maybe we might have another conversation somewhere down the line."

"*Jah,* I don't see why not," he said with a grin so sunny it made Anna feel like the sun had briefly appeared in the night sky. "I'm an easy man to find. Most days, you'll find me working out in my fields. You're more than welcome to seek me out there if it's not distasteful."

"*Nee*, certainly not!" she assured him, unable to keep her mouth from breaking open into a smile so wide it hurt her face. "I can't think of any place lovelier to have a conversation than in *Gott's* big, beautiful world."

Caleb nodded, and although he didn't say anything more, she had a feeling that he was pleased with the answer. She was pleased as well, pleased with the entire situation. As she walked slowly back towards her *haus*, she felt the first stirrings of real, undeniable hope sparking in her heart.

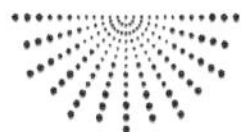

CHAPTER FIVE

And we know that in all things
God works for the good of those who love him,
who have been called according to his purpose.
Romans 8:28

As Anna sunk into sleep that night, she felt not even a hint of the shame she had felt in the barn. The rejection in the barn might as well have taken place in a different lifetime. Even though she was sure, she would never actually seek Caleb again; the fact that he'd seemed eager to have another talk with her made her feel like the luckiest woman in the world. For the first time in her entire life, she felt as though she had really, truly been seen.

And, over the course of the next several weeks, she managed to surprise herself. Despite being sure that she would not make her way to Caleb's farm, two days after he walked her home, she found herself standing beside his fence. It was as though her feet had carried her there of her own volition, prepared to make up for the confidence she lacked.

She had been so nervous that first time that she had promised herself never to return again, but Caleb had seen her standing there and set aside his work. After their talk, she had gone away feeling as though she could walk on the very air itself, and she had come back to visit several times since then.

She had always believed that if she spent too much time with anyone outside of her immediate *familye,* especially a member of the opposite sex, they would eventually grow tired of her. She hadn't thought it would take very long, either, which was something she had expressed to her *mamm* and *schweschder* many times before.

Now, she was surprised and utterly delighted to find that her fears were not coming to fruition. Unless she was very much mistaken, or unless Caleb was highly skilled at hiding his true feelings about a thing, this *wunderbaar* man appeared to truly enjoy her company. It was one of those things that fell under the umbrella of too good to be true, and yet every time he smiled at her, she felt their closeness grow.

"What is it, Anna?" he asked now, his voice thick with rich laughter. "Where did you go just now?"

"*Ach,* nowhere," she replied with a blush, something she did quite often when in Caleb's company. "I was just thinking about how different it is for me to spend time with you than it is when I try to spend time with others."

"Is that so?" Caleb asked, wiping away a light sheen of sweat with the back of one strong, muscled-forearm. "What do you mean?"

"When I'm with other people, with most people, really, I feel so out of place," Anna said, frowning in a way that made Caleb smile as she tried to get to the bottom of what exactly it was that she wanted to say. "I feel like I'm a million miles away, or perhaps like

I'm trapped somewhere underwater, and nothing I say can help me get back up to the surface. I know I'm not making any sense..."

"*Nee,* I wouldn't say that," he corrected her gently, the look in his eyes making her think that he wanted her to go on. "I think I understand what you're trying to get at."

"It's just that my interests don't seem to be the same as the other people near my age," Anna continued in a rush of words that felt as though they had been trying to escape her lips for time eternal. "Where they want to laugh and play, and sometimes even get up to mischief, my interests go towards the quieter things in life. It oftentimes makes me feel like I'm on the outskirts of everything. Almost like I'm an *Englischer* or something."

"*Ach,* believe me, Anna, I understand," Caleb said with a smile that wasn't quite able to cover up the momentary sadness that flickered in his eyes. "More than you know."

"But, Caleb, surely not," Anna protested, then clamped a hand over her mouth briefly as she tried to understand what on earth would have made her say something so bold. "Or, all I mean to say is that you seem so happy and easy to get along with. Even the fact that you volunteered to chaperone the game night where we met. It makes me think that you must enjoy people at least a little bit."

"*Ach,* that game night," Caleb said with a chuckle and a shake of the head. "I can see why you might have gotten that impression, but being a part of that wasn't really my idea. I'm not sure you could even go so far as to say that I volunteered."

"*Ach,* Caleb!" Anna laughed, almost light-headed with how good that simple act felt. "I have *nee* idea what that's supposed to mean!"

"It means that my being there in the first place was an idea of Bishop Amos Beiler's," Caleb said with a shrug. "When left to my own devices, I prefer a good, hard day's work and a simple night at home to the more exciting prospect of social pursuits. It was Amos who nudged me to 'get myself out of my shell.' It's not something I would ever have done on my own."

"Do you think he was right?" Anna asked, suddenly unsure of herself and their conversation.

"I do," Caleb answered with a nod and a contemplative expression in his hazel eyes.

"Well, then I think I must say that I'm sorry," she said, lowering her eyes the way she had done the first time they had spoken. "Looking after me and walking me home, that must have kept you from getting to meet more people at the gathering. Surely, that was what you were hoping for, was it not?"

"I don't know what I was hoping for, but I know you shouldn't be sorry," Caleb said, looking at her with a level of intensity that left her breathless. "What was it that you said that first night? That you had *nee* regrets?"

"That's right," she said with a nod, part of her wanting to throw her hands up in the air and jump for joy at the discovery that her words mattered enough to Caleb for him to remember them even weeks after she had spoken them.

"Well, I don't have any regrets, either," Caleb continued, lifting a hesitant hand and allowing it to hover in the air between them before placing it lightly on her shoulder. "I think that *Gott* put us there together for a reason, and I, for one, am so glad.

Meeting you and the subsequent time we've spent together has brought me more joy over the last several weeks than I've known since my Esther passed away. I never expected to feel that again."

His hand moved from her shoulder to her cheek as he allowed one rough, calloused thumb to trace the line of her jaw lightly. She shuddered and trembled, asking herself if she could really say what she longed to say next.

"Do you ever think about it, Caleb?" she asked, almost swallowing the words before they could make their way into the world.

"Do I think about what, Anna?" he asked with low intensity, unlike anything she had heard from him before.

"About getting married again," she whispered, her lips numb with terror and disbelief at what they were saying. "It's probably a terrible thing for me to think about, let alone to ask, but..."

"I never did," he interrupted, running a thumb along her cheek before finally dropping his hand. "Before."

"Before what?" she asked breathlessly.

There was a part of her that was sure she already knew the answer, but a larger part of her wouldn't allow herself to believe that it was true. The extent to which she had already gotten her hopes up was dangerous indeed. But to entertain the fantasy, she was concocting now? Having that picked apart was a devastation she was sure she wouldn't be able to bear.

"Before I met you," he said with a half-smile. "All of that started to change when I met you."

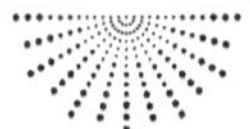

CHAPTER SIX

I keep my eyes always on the Lord.
With him at my right hand, I will not be shaken.
Psalm 16:8

It was a week after Caleb's revelation, and Anna still felt as though her whole body was shot through with electricity. Their conversation was with her all of the time, making her smile and sometimes even giggle for *nee* real reason at all. It was the last thing she thought about when she laid down to sleep at night and the first thing that popped into her head when she awoke the next day.

"All of that started to change when I met you," she would whisper to herself, her eyes filling with tears of happiness, a truly novel experience for her.

Although they spoke on the matter *nee* further, she and Caleb arranged to have a supper together, one that would be held at her *familye haus*. When first they spoke of it, Anna had felt like the time would never come, and yet now, it was only an hour or so until Caleb was supposed to arrive.

With her heart racing at the thought of his impending arrival, she flitted around the kitchen, overseeing details of the supper that she had already tended to a half a dozen times before. She was so tightly wound that when Ruth snuck into the kitchen behind her, she let out a little shriek and jumped about a foot in the air.

"You really shouldn't sneak up on people like that," she scolded, although she was in far too good of a mood to truly be annoyed. "Haven't I told you that before?"

"You have," Ruth answered sulkily, her arms folded

tightly across her chest as she surveyed the room with a distasteful expression on her usually serene face. "But that's not what I'm trying to do."

"All right, then what are you trying to do?" Anna asked, doing her best to be light-hearted in the face of her *schweschder's* most unusual temper.

"Honestly?" Ruth answered, moving further into the room and taking a seat at the small kitchen table in the corner. "I came to ask you why you're doing this."

"What do you mean?" Anna asked with a frown, although she had a sneaking suspicion that she already knew what Ruth was going to say. "I'm not sure what you're talking about."

"I'm talking about this," Ruth repeated with a sigh, gesturing at the feast of food sitting on the counters and waiting to be transferred to the table. "All of this. Why are you going to all of this trouble, Anna? All of this for that old man?"

"Really, Ruth!" Anna gasped, shocked at how uncharitable her younger *schweschder* was being. "What an unkind thing to say! Besides, he's not an old man at all. He's only a couple of years older than me."

"Fine, but I still don't see what all of the fuss is about," Ruth insisted, her hands balled up into fists by her side. "I don't understand why he's coming to supper at all."

Anna sighed and looked out the window, trying to collect herself before she tackled Ruth's question. Despite being so dissimilar, the two of them had always gotten along famously. Ever since Anna and Caleb had started spending time together, however, there seemed to be a wedge between them. It hurt Anna's heart to feel it, but it confused her as well. Her *familye* had always seemed so worried about her happiness and well-being. But now, when she was happier than she could ever recall being in her life, they seemed doubtful. Anna sensed that more in Ruth than in anyone else, and it made her sick to her stomach with regret.

"He's coming to supper because we're friends," she answered, lifting her chin definitely and practically daring Ruth to argue further. "He makes me happy, Ruth, and that should be enough for the rest of you."

Ruth opened her mouth as if to say something more, and then promptly shut it again. Whatever doubt lingered in her mind, she was apparently content on letting it rest for the moment.

Anna remained troubled by the disconnect between her and her *schweschder,* but she chose to put it aside in her mind in favor of her excitement at seeing Caleb again. By the time she heard the knock at the front door, she had tucked her sadness in the corner of her mind where it would not be able to ruin her evening.

"Well, hello there," Anna's *daed* said as he opened the door. "You must be Caleb."

"That's right," Caleb said with a smile and a nod.

"My name is Matthias, and my *fraa* here is Leah," her father continued, stepping aside and gesturing for Caleb to enter the *haus.* "We're pleased to have you here."

Caleb came inside, and Leah hurried forward to shut the door. She glanced at Caleb with frank curiosity, her expression betraying nothing of her immediate opinion of the man. If she felt as strongly about him as Ruth did, however, that feeling did not show.

After some slightly awkward conversation, the five of

them sat down at the supper table. In the middle of the table was a lovely, fragrant bouquet of flowers that Caleb had delivered to Anna upon his arrival. Caleb sat across from Anna, and every time she peered at the friendly blooms, she caught a glimpse of him smiling at her sweetly.

Anna was petrified that Ruth's unexplainable poor opinion of Caleb, and subsequently, of Anna's judgment, would poison the entire get together. As the meal progressed, however, she realized that her worrying was for nothing, and she was able to let her guard down a little as she felt Caleb do the same.

It was true that Ruth made *nee* attempt to get to know Caleb better, choosing instead to shift her food around her plate listlessly. But she made *nee* trouble, either, and Anna's parents both seemed to warm to Caleb as the minute hand of the clock ticked by.

"Well, I'll admit," her *daed* said now, looking at Anna as if he could read her relief written across her face. "I had my reservations about you coming here."

"Please," Anna whispered, almost too low for anyone to hear.

She did not wish to speak out of turn, nor to

challenge her father's authority, but she dreaded what he might say next. So, too, did she dread what Caleb might make of it.

"I can understand why," Caleb said, his tone soothing and his expression remaining untroubled. "I think that if I ever have a *dochder,* it will be difficult for me to let any stranger look at her, let alone spend time with her."

"It's true, I feel that way," Matthias said, nodding approvingly and looking at Anna with clear affection. "But mostly I worry that people be kind to her. They haven't always been, you know, and the pain it has caused her has pained me as well."

"And more's the pity for them not to get to know how *wunderbaar* she is," Caleb said earnestly, his eyes clouding a little at the mention of any past cruelties she may have suffered. "But, also, I would like to see to it that nobody ever treats her unkindly again. Not if I can help it."

"That's very gallant of you," Anna's mother spoke up quickly, her eyes flitting back and forth between Caleb's face and Anna's. "But what exactly is it that you're trying to say?"

"I'm trying, and I fear doing a bad job of it, to tell you that your *dochder* has brought light back into my life. I never thought I would want to marry again, but now it's the only thing I can think about. With your permission, Matthias, I would dearly love to take Anna for my *fraa*."

There was a moment of stunned silence so complete that it seemed to Anna as though time had stopped. Caleb sat perfectly still, never taking his hopeful eyes off of her daed's face. Her parents looked searchingly at each other, trying to have a conversation about this unexpected turn of events using only their eyes. Ruth had eyes only for Caleb, and in them, Anna saw nothing of the friendly, loving girl she knew to be her *schweschder*.

"Please," Anna said again, standing abruptly and trying to look at everyone all at once. "I know how much all of you have worried about me, about my happiness and what was to become of me as I grew older. I used to worry about it, too, but it hasn't once crossed my mind since meeting Caleb. I can be happy with him, *Daed*. I will be so terribly happy as his *fraa*."

For a terrible moment that could have been as long as

eternity, the silence amongst Anna's *familye* persisted. She was just starting to fear that her one chance at happiness would be taken away before she could have it when her *daed* nodded, some internal debate apparently decided.

"If you want to make her happy and to keep her safe," he said gruffly, although his eyes betrayed a wealth of emotion, Anna knew he would never be able to express. "Then our desires for my Anna are the same. If she wishes to accept your proposal, then the two of you may be wed with my blessing."

"And with mine," Anna's mother chimed in, her eyes shining with happy tears.

The silence dissolved then, as everyone else got up from their chairs while they all spoke at once. Anna was embraced first by Caleb, with whom she had never had such close physical contact and which left her feeling as breathless as if she had run several miles.

Next came her parents, who both wiped happy tears away from their cheeks as they told her how pleased they were that she had found the path *Gott* had set out before her. It was only when Anna turned to

Ruth, the last to approach her, that she realized the mood in the room was not a universally happy one.

"Won't you embrace me, *schweschder*?" Anna asked uncertainly when Ruth kept her arms folded tightly across her chest. "Aren't you happy for me?"

"Of course, I'll embrace you," Ruth said in a wooden voice entirely unlike her usual, lively cadence. She made *nee* attempt at answering the second question at all. "So, you really mean to do this?"

"Why, *jah*," Anna said quickly, letting Ruth go and stepping back as if she'd been stung. "Why wouldn't I?"

As Anna took another, faltering step backward, she ran directly into Caleb, who had to rest his hands on her shoulders to keep her upright. It was then that Anna realized that Ruth's icy stare was meant for Caleb and Caleb alone.

For whatever reason, and the origins of this Anna could not fathom, Ruth was not prepared to share in Anna's joyous news. She was not happy for them, not happy at all.

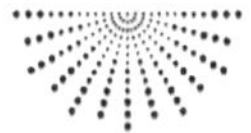

*5 Trust in the LORD with all your heart
and lean not on your own understanding;
6 in all your ways submit to him,
and he will make your paths straight.
Proverbs 3:5-6*

Later, when Anna finally had a moment to breathe and for the excitement to settle a little, she would start thinking of her life in two parts. There was the first act, in which Anna was sure that she would always feel separated and alone.

This was all she had come to expect from life, and the fate she had resigned herself to.

Now, however, there was the second part, and this she was sure would always feel just a little bit like a dream. She actually had to pinch herself as she lay in bed that first night, reminding herself again and again that Caleb's proposal was real. She was *nee* longer fated to walk the world alone. *Gott* had put her in the path of the person she had been meant to be with all along.

She worried at the start that her *mamm* might not be as excited as she, instead choosing to hold onto her initial reservations. She had dreamed and longed for this day for such a long time, despite being sure that it would never happen, that the idea of her mamm being unable to share her joy was a retched one indeed.

Fortunately, Leah Sutter seemed to be at least as excited as Anna was herself. The very next morning after Caleb's proposal, Anna descended the stairs from her room to find not only her *mamm* waiting for her but Sarah Beiler as well.

"*Ach,* hello!" Sarah cried, throwing her hands up into

the air with delight and getting to her feet. "I must say, your *mamm* has been dying to go upstairs and wake you. She's been very eager to start."

"It's true," Leah said, her cheeks rosy and her expression merry. "I won't even try to deny it. All I could think about last night was the fact that you are to become a *fraa*. You just seem so... well, so happy, my darling *dochder*."

"*Denke*," Anna said with a low, gentle laugh. "I'm very happy. I feel very blessed. Although to be perfectly honest, I'm not sure I completely understand what's happening right now."

"We're going to plan your wedding!" Sarah said happily, taking her seat again and patting a space beside her on the couch so that Anna would join them. "And there's *nee* time to start like the present."

I t wasn't only that first morning that Sarah came to help Anna and her *mamm* with the planning of the impending event. Sometimes, it felt to Anna as if the bishop's *fraa* had taken up part-time residence in the Sutter *haus*, which pleased her *nee* end.

She had always liked Sarah, but it was more than that. As the three of them planned, Anna was undeniably the center of attention. It was something that she would have shied away from just a month before, and yet now, she was able to appreciate it for what it was. Caleb's proposal had planted in her the seed of confidence needed for her to believe that she was just as worthy as any other resident of Faith's Creek. It was something that was growing into a new self-assurance, and that was something she very much hoped would be a permanent change.

The only dark spot in the happiness of her planning was Ruth's insistent refusal to participate in any of it. She spent more time out of the *haus* than she had ever done before, choosing to spend time with Jonathan and her friends instead of sharing in Anna's joy. It was as if Anna's choice to accept Caleb's proposal had somehow put an end to the first friendship Anna had ever had.

Still, every time the front door opened and Ruth came inside, Anna's heart leaped with the hope that this time, Ruth would come around. She imagined that Ruth would sink sheepishly into the sitting room where Anna, their *mamm,* and Sarah planned, and ask if she could be a part of things, after all.

She imagined it so many times that when Ruth finally stepped into the room, not slinking but with a manic expression on her face that made Anna feel cold all over, a part of Anna didn't believe it was real. She blinked rapidly, half-sure that when her vision cleared, Ruth would be there *nee* longer.

"*Ach,* darling," their *mamm* said happily, although Anna imagined that she heard just a hint of hesitation there. "I'm so glad that you're here. Sarah has come again to help with the preparations. Perhaps you would like to join us this time?"

"*Nee,*" Ruth said quickly, and without so much as a glance in their visitor's direction. "I don't want to help with anything. When I tell you what I've come here to say, I don't think you'll want to continue with the planning anyway."

"Please, Ruth," Anna objected weakly, shaking her head from side to side as if the motion alone would be enough to stop whatever was about to come.

"Don't. Can't you just be happy for me? You know that I will be for you when the time comes."

"He has *familye* in Ohio, *Mamm*, did you know that?" Ruth went on, steadfastly refusing to look at Anna or heed her pleas. "Caleb does, I mean. He's got people in Ohio, and they've got a lot of money that Caleb stands to inherit someday."

"What are you going on about, Ruth?" their *mamm* asked dismissively, although there was a flicker of unease on her face. "Come, sit. Help us see that everything is ready."

"*Nee*, I won't do that!" Ruth replied, stamping her foot in a display of temper almost entirely foreign to her typically genial demeanor. "I won't, because this wedding shouldn't happen. He didn't ask her because he loves her and wants her to be his *fraa, Mamm*. He asked her because he wants to get that money!"

This was met by a stunned, sick silence so profound that Anna wondered if she had gone deaf. Not that she would have been able to hear a word spoken, anyway. The blood was rushing too loudly in her ears for her to listen to anything but its angry movement. She hardly even noticed when their *mamm* began to speak.

"Ruth, that's enough," she demanded, her face as white as a sheet and her expression full of reprimand. "If you can't be happy for your *schweschder*..."

"I'm not making it up," Ruth interrupted, insistent on being heard even in the face of their *mamm's* severe disapproval. "Jonathan overheard his parents talking about it, and he came straight over to tell me. Caleb only gets his inheritance money if he has an heir. *Nee* wonder he wants to take a new, young *fraa*. He wants our Anna so that she can produce the *kinner* he needs to get his money."

Anna never made a conscious decision to flee. Her feet just seemed to move of their own volition, carrying her out of the room and stumbling up the stairs. Her body was trying to return her to safety, even as her mind reeled and struggled to comprehend what she had just learned.

Behind her, there was a wealth of noise. There came the sounds of Anna's *mamm* scolding Ruth for participating and perpetrating idle gossip, with Ruth insisting that she was doing nothing of the sort. It didn't sound like the kind of argument that was going to reach resolution anytime soon.

So, too, could Anna hear Sarah hurrying after her, trying to coax Anna down the stairs again so that they could get to the bottom of what surely must be a terrible misunderstanding.

None of this noise mattered to Anna, and she did not turn around. She would not stop for anyone or anything now, not when it felt as though her life depended on reaching the solitude of her bedroom.

It felt like it took an eternity to get there, although some distant, still-rational part of her brain understood that the entire scene could only have taken a couple of minutes to unfold. Still, when she reached her room, she slammed the door behind her, bolting it before collapsing onto her bed into a writhing, miserable heap.

As the sobs overtook her, she knew that what Ruth had said had to be true. It was the only thing that made sense. She was not the kind of woman that a man could love, and she had been a fool ever to think otherwise.

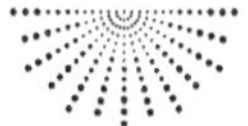

CHAPTER EIGHT

28 "Come to me, all you who are weary and burdened, and I will give you rest. 29 Take my yoke upon you and learn from me, for I am gentle and humble in heart, and you will find rest for your souls. 30 For my yoke is easy and my burden is light."

Matthew 11:28-30

It was a full day before Caleb realized that anything was wrong, and even then, part of him wanted to go on insisting that it wasn't so. After all, since his proposal and the commencement of the wedding planning, he had seen a good deal less of Anna.

Although he missed her company terribly, he understood. She was with her *mamm* and *schweschder*, which was as it should be at a time like this. She was happy, and that was the only thing that mattered to him in the world.

He first became aware that there was something more diabolical at work than just Anna being busy when he made a trip into the town's general store to pick up some supplies. Always before, he had been greeted with friendliness and generosity. Now, people whispered as he passed, giving him looks as though they were looking at the worst kind of villain.

Although nobody was willing to speak to him directly about what the trouble was, gossip traveled quickly, and especially in towns as small as Faith's Creek. Before long, he understood just how terrible the rumors about him racing through the district truly were. It made him sick to his stomach, and he pushed all thoughts except for getting to Anna roughly aside.

He raced through town and down the road upon

which he had first discovered his fondness for Anna, his heart hammering nauseatingly at the bottom of his throat. By the time he arrived at the Sutter *haus*, he felt as though he would never have enough air in his lungs again.

He pulled his fist up before the door to knock, then hesitated, swallowing hard as he considered what he might find on the other side. He did not know for a fact that Anna had heard the rumors about his reasons for wanting to marry her, for he had *nee* proof that she had heard anything at all. He felt it in his bones, however, and the prospect of facing her and her *familye* to try to convince them of the truth seemed a daunting task indeed.

"And one I must take on," he growled to himself, squaring his shoulders and preparing to knock once again. "I love her, and I cannot let her go."

He rapped quickly on the door, then took a step backward and held his hands clasped loosely before him. His heart was racing at an uncomfortable pace, but he was careful not to let his nerves show on his face. If ever before, he had needed to present himself as confident and trustworthy, surely it was now.

"You," Matthias said by way of greeting, opening the front door just enough to glare out at Caleb. "I was wondering how long it would take for you to show your face here. It's a wonder that you could do it at all, after the way you've used my girl."

"*Nee*, Matthias, please," Caleb said, holding both of his hands out in what he hoped was a placating gesture. "It's not like that. I've just now heard what's being said about me in town, and..."

"Do you know where she's been, ever since her *schweschder* came home with the news?" Matthias interrupted, the vein in his forehead standing out in alarming prominence. "She's been up in her room, crying. I hear her at all hours, and she won't let herself be consoled. She won't let anyone near her, Caleb, and it's all because of you."

"*Ach, nee*," Caleb tried again, although he could feel himself growing weaker by the moment, and he already knew his words alone were never going to be enough to convince Anna's father of his innocence. "You don't understand."

"I understand enough," Matthias said solemnly, and in a way that made it clear to Caleb that he was done for. "I understand that you aren't welcome on my property any longer. I want you to leave now, Caleb, and don't trouble our *dochder* again. You've caused her more than enough pain as it is."

Caleb was afforded *nee* opportunity to speak further or to defend himself. Before he could so much as draw another breath, Matthias shut the door in his face, leaving Caleb standing in front of the door like a fool.

He trudged back down the road slowly, feeling as though all of the strength had leached out of his body. He didn't care if the whole of Faith's Creek treated him as an outcast, just so long as Anna loved him. But to lose her now, when he was so close to a life full of love and happiness again? That was a wound he did not think he could bear.

He didn't make a conscious decision to visit Bishop Beiler's *haus*; rather, his body seemed to bring him there without giving his mind any say in the matter. It was as though he had traveled there in a nightmare, one from which he wasn't sure he would ever be able to wake up.

"Well, hello," Amos greeted him, opening his door

before Caleb could get all of the way up the walk. "It's good to see you, Caleb."

"Is it?" Caleb asked, laughing with a bitterness he did not know he possessed. "If so, you're the only one who thinks so."

"All right," Amos said smoothly, registering *nee* surprise at hearing Caleb's dark mood. "I think you'd better come inside, don't you? I'm sure that whatever is the matter is nothing that a strong cup of *kaffe* and a good conversation can't fix."

Caleb doubted that very much, but he appreciated the sentiment and was more grateful than he could say to be invited into somebody's home. He had a feeling he wasn't going to see much of that in the district from this point on.

"So, what brings you here?" Amos asked once the two of them had settled in at the kitchen table, two steaming mugs of black *kaffe,* and two pieces of chocolate cake had been placed before them.

"Surely you must know, Amos," Caleb said, his voice hoarse and cracking with emotion. "I think all of Faith's Creek has heard the rumors about me by now."

"I have," Amos said with a nod, although he didn't look uncomfortable in the least, which impressed Caleb despite his despair. "But I don't like to assume I know a man's business before he speaks his mind. And, for what it's worth, rumors don't carry any weight with me. I'm only interested in the truth."

"If it's the truth you want, I do have *familye* in Ohio, and there is money to be had," Caleb said, rubbing his temples gingerly with the tips of his fingers. "But that's the only part of the rumor that's true. That inheritance was the last thing on my mind when I asked Anna to marry me. I want her to be my *fraa* because I love her. I want us to build a life together, to take care of her. I want us to take care of each other, to have an equal partnership. I don't care if we never see a dime of the money my *familye* has. Nothing could matter less to me."

Caleb was out of breath by the time he finished talking, and he was surprised that the impassioned speech had come from him in the first place. He'd thought he was too stunned by the sudden change of events to articulate his desires at all, and he was pleased to find that in that, at least, he was wrong.

"I'll tell you plainly," Amos said after considering

Caleb's words for a good, long while. "That I believe you. I've seen men in love before, and I know the look."

"And I appreciate that, but it doesn't matter unless Anna and her *familye* believe it," Caleb said, dangerously close to tears now.

"You're right about that," Amos said, nodding his head and watching Caleb with eyes that were full of compassion. "And so you must make them believe."

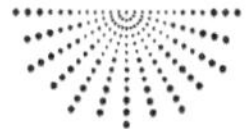

CHAPTER NINE

So do not fear, for I am with you;
do not be dismayed, for I am your God.
I will strengthen you and help you;
I will uphold you with my righteous right hand.
Isaiah 41:10

"*Ach*, come on, Anna! You can't just sit here in your room for the rest of your life. You can't just remain on your own day after day. People are meant to be with each other. We're meant to form connections, right?"

Anna responded with a sound that was caught somewhere in between a laugh and a sob. She never bothered to pull her gaze away from the little window she sat beside. She felt like she had been sitting there for all of her life, and she couldn't imagine ever moving again.

It had been almost two weeks, by her estimation, since Ruth had come home and delivered the news that had destroyed Anna's life. She had hardly left her room since that time, choosing to keep herself rooted to her chair and looking out her window into the world she would never be a part of again.

It felt as though she was keeping vigil, mourning her own death. Because surely a part of her had died upon hearing what Ruth had to say. Nothing less than death could possibly have hurt as much as she had at that moment, and continued to feel now, both when awake and when asleep.

"Please, Anna, can't you try?" Ruth pressed, practically hopping into Anna's line of sight to force her attention. "It will start to get better if you do. You'll start to feel like yourself again, and I bet it will happen sooner than you think. Maybe if you come to another afternoon of games with me, you'll spend some time outside again, and you'll see that it's not all so bad."

Anna almost laughed at what Ruth was proposing in the seconds it took for her to realize that her younger *schweschder* was serious. Then, she could only stare, the suggestion and everything it implied was so terrible that she was rendered speechless.

What words was she supposed to use to explain that her heart *nee* longer beat for her, although it still resided inside of her chest? How was she supposed to make Ruth, who had always been so pretty and easily accepted everywhere she went, understand what it felt like to lose the only life she had ever really wanted?

"*Nee*, Ruth," she finally said, painfully aware that any attempts at explaining her thoughts and pain would fall woefully short. "I won't accompany you to the games this afternoon. I won't ever go to a gathering like that again. I... I can't. I don't want to."

Ruth nodded, although she couldn't hide her disappointment. There was something more than disappointment, too, something that almost looked like fear. When she met Anna's eyes, there were tears glistening in her long, dark lashes.

"Are you angry with me, Anna?" she asked in a small, child-like voice that Anna could remember from when they were smaller, and Ruth had thought she had finally pushed her too far. "For what I told you? Do you... do you hate me?"

Anna took a moment to consider the question. Ruth deserved an honest answer, at the very least, and Anna wanted to know the answer as well. For a moment, she was afraid that the bond between her and her *schweschder* was broken in a way that could never be repaired. It was true that *nee* matter what else happened between them, Ruth would always be the one who had delivered the death blow to Anna's happy relationship. She had gone looking for it, too. She had gone in search of proof that Caleb couldn't possibly love Anna for who she was.

"*Nee,*" Anna finally answered with a weary smile, weighing all of these things and finding that her love for Ruth mattered more than all of the rest of it. "I don't hate you, *schweschder,* and I never could. But I also can't pretend that everything is perfectly fine. I can't just erase Caleb from my heart just because you want me to be better. I won't ever be able to..."

She was going to tell Anna that she would never be able to recover from this pain when a loud, pounding noise startled them both, even bringing Anna to her feet. She and Ruth stood very still, their heads straining towards the open door to hear what new trouble had come to find them.

"Please, Matthias, I understand that you're angry," a voice rang out as clear as a bell, even through the thick wood of the still latched door. "But I've brought what you need. I've brought proof that the ugly rumors going around about me in town aren't true."

"Caleb!" Anna cried breathlessly at the same time as Ruth put out an arm to keep her in place.

"*Nee*, Anna," Ruth said, although her voice was full of doubt, and her eyes were as wide as saucers. "Don't. Let *Daed* take care of it. He'll send him on his way. He'll make him understand that he can't do this to you anymore. He needs to leave you in peace."

"And what if he really does have something to say?" Anna demanded, speaking more forcefully now than she could ever remember speaking in her life. "What if what you heard is wrong, and he has a way to prove it?"

"I know you want it to be that way, but how could it be possible?" Ruth asked, her lower lip trembling as her hands twisted in fretful knots in front of her. "*Daed* knows best, don't you think?"

"That may be true," Anna replied over her shoulder as she strode purposefully for the door. "But I know Caleb. Or at least I think I do, and I want to hear what he's come to say."

She descended the stairs carefully, afraid that her trembling legs would give out on her and leave her tumbling down the stairs. She moved with purpose, though, and her *daed* heard her coming before she had even reached the bottom step.

"It's all right, my girl," he said, his eyes bright with worry and his brow furrowed into a frown. "I'll take care of it. I'll send him on his way and make sure that he knows not to come back again."

"*Nee*, please," she said softly, pleased to find that her voice didn't shake as violently as did her knees. "Don't do that, at least not yet. I want to hear what he has to say."

"Are you sure?" he asked uncertainly as Anna's *mamm* hurried into the front hall and stood close by. "I don't want him to hurt you more than he already has."

"I'm sure," she said, lifting her chin defiantly. "I love him, *Daed*, and I don't think that will ever stop. If there's a chance for us, or at least for some kind of closure, I have to take it."

Her *daed* hesitated for several seconds longer before nodding reluctantly and going to the door. He opened it slowly as if waiting for her to change her mind and tell him to shut it again. When he realized that it wasn't going to happen, he shook his head and opened it further, glaring out at Caleb with hard, distrustful eyes.

"*Denke*," Caleb said quietly, nodding at Matthias to show his appreciation. "*Denke*, for being willing to listen."

"It wasn't my idea," Anna's *daed* replied, his words wooden and unhappy. "It's Anna who is allowing this to happen. If you do or say anything to hurt her, you'll be told to leave again, and this time it will be for good."

"Understood," Caleb said, stepping inside of the *haus* with his shoulders squared and a quiet dignity about his person. "If I think for one moment that I'm causing her further pain, I'll see myself out. All I want to do is look after her heart."

Anna could see that her *daed* had plenty more that he wanted to say on the subject, but she stepped forward, shaking her head and stopping him before he could speak again. She didn't even have to look at him to do it, either, which was a very good thing. After two weeks and everything that had happened, she only had eyes for Caleb.

"Caleb?" she said his name in both greeting and question, a plea for some sort of explanation for all of the terrible things she had heard about him.

"I'm sorry, Anna," he said, shaking his head sadly. "Truly, I am. If I'd had any idea that people would learn about my *familye* in Ohio and twist it in such a terrible way..."

"But how do we know they're twisting anything?" Ruth demanded, the edge of mistrust still firmly in place in her voice.

"I've brought what proof I can," he said humbly,

reaching inside of his coat pocket and pulling out an envelope that had been folded many times. "All I can do is hope that it will be enough."

He held the envelope out in front of him like an offering, but before Anna could take it, her *daed* snatched it up, his hands shaking as he opened the flap and pulled out a letter. He read a couple of lines, and then nudged Anna's *mamm,* motioning for her to read along with him. When they were done, they both looked up at Caleb with disbelief.

"Is this true, Caleb?" her *mamm* asked, with just the smallest hint of hopefulness creeping into her voice. "Is this real?"

"It is," Caleb answered with a nod, daring to inch a little further into the room, and several steps closer to where Anna stood rooted to the floor. "Amos knows of the *familye,* too, if you'd be more comfortable checking with him."

"Is what true?" Anna asked, for once too impatient to wait to have her say. "What does the letter say?"

"It's from my uncle," Caleb said, his warm eyes burning into hers so that she could not possibly look away. "I wrote to him and told him that I don't want any part of that money, whether I have a *kinner* or not. It's something I should have done long ago, only I didn't see the point after Esther died. If I'd had any idea the kind of damage, it would do..."

"You did that?" Anna asked, struggling to keep both her breath and her heartbeat steady. "You gave that up, just like that?"

"Of course I did," he replied, everything about him pleading with her to hear his words and to believe. "And I would give up a good deal more. I would do just about anything if it meant that I could have you as my *fraa*."

There were more words to be spoken between them and to be had between Caleb and Anna's *familye* as well. There would be time for that later, though, because now they had as much time as they could need. As Anna raced towards him, allowing him to pull her into a fierce embrace, she understood that her happiness was still waiting for her, after all.

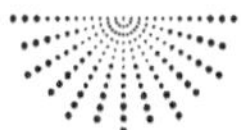

CHAPTER TEN

⁶ Do not be anxious about anything,
but in every situation, by prayer and petition,
with thanksgiving, present your requests to God.
⁷ And the peace of God, which transcends all
understanding,
will guard your hearts and your minds in Christ
Jesus.
Philippians 4:6-7

nna and Caleb's wedding was held one short month later, with both of them eager to put those dark days of separation behind them. They were painful to think about, and there seemed to be an unspoken consensus between the pair that they wanted to start their new lives together as soon as possible.

Still, Anna couldn't quite make herself regret what happened. As terrible as it was, it had allowed her to see Caleb's true colors, and to understand the depth of his love for her. If there was anything she wished she could change, it was how easily she had succumbed to her doubts. It made her sad to think that she might have let Caleb down before the two of them were even wed.

"I thought I might find you here," Caleb's rich, playful voice spoke up from behind where she stood on the back porch, watching the bustle of pre-wedding activity. "A little birdie told me that the porch is where you go to think."

"Would that little birdie be my *mamm*?" she asked with a happy smile, leaving behind her melancholy thoughts.

"*Nee,* actually," he said, coming up beside her and standing so close that she could feel his warmth. "It was Ruth."

"*Ach,*" Anna said slowly, considering for a moment before she continued, finally voicing the thing that had been troubling her. "That was kind of her. And I'm glad you brought her up, actually. I don't think I've ever properly told you how sorry I am."

"Sorry?" he asked with surprise. "You? But for what?"

"Well, for doubting you," she said, her lower lip beginning to tremble. "For believing what Ruth and everyone else had to say so easily. I should have given you the benefit of the doubt. I should have come to you, talked to you, instead of shutting myself away and believing what I was told."

"Never be sorry for that," he said earnestly, moving a hand to her face and stroking the side of her cheek gently. "I should have been more upfront with you about everything. I'm only glad that I found a way to make things right."

"But that's just it," Anna insisted, lifting a hand to place over his and looking deep into his eyes. "You shouldn't have had to do that. You shouldn't have been forced to make a sacrifice for my sake."

"That's the thing about sacrifices," he said with a deep chuckle as he pulled her in even closer. "Nobody can really make you do them, and especially not when they're made for the right reasons. If you have to think of it as a sacrifice, which I most certainly do not, think of it as a sacrifice for love. Surely, there can be *nee* greater kind."

"And you don't resent me?" Anna asked, even as her last shreds of anxiety melted away. "Me, or my *familye*? With the way they treated you, with how all of us behaved. I wouldn't blame you if you did. But if you do, you should tell me now. Harboring resentment is *nee* way to enter a marriage."

"You're right about that," Caleb said with a smile. "And fortunately for us, I have none. If there's anything more I want to say before we become man and *fraa*, it's *denke*."

"*Denke*?" she echoed with a disbelieving laugh. "But for what? I don't think I did anything deserving of that."

"But you did," he said softly, kissing the top of her *kapp*-clad head. "You believed in me when it mattered the most, and you helped your *familye* to come around to trusting me, too. You've given me a life again when I thought it was all but done."

"And with any luck, we'll have a *boppli* of our own soon," Anna added shyly, hardly able to believe that she was in a position to speak those words. "We'll build a *familye* together, and the love will grow with us, too."

Caleb bent and kissed the tip of her nose, then pulled back from her with a boyish grin spread widely across his face. He had never looked as handsome before as he did at that moment. His smile was enough to put all concerns about resentment to rest once and for all.

The two of them remained on the porch together for a few moments more before joining the crowd of people who had all come to celebrate with them.

As Anna walked with Caleb's arm around her waist, she realized that she had never felt so content or so much herself in her whole life. It was love that had given that to her, *Gott's* greatest gift of all. Moving forward, she knew that she would never doubt that again.

As Ruth stood on the back porch of her *familye* home peering out at the world, she could not help but think of her older *schweschder,* Anna. It was not so very long ago that Anna could be found in this exact spot, working tirelessly and spending almost all of her time alone.

"And I used to tease her for it," Ruth reminded herself softly, shaking her head at the memory of careless comments she had made. However, she had meant them as playful at the time. "So it serves me right, to be standing here in her stead now. It's what I deserve, and likely not near enough."

The thought made her both sad and sorry for herself. It was a feeling she had become accustomed to of late. For most of her life, she had been the most carefree kind of girl, but those days felt like a very long time ago now.

The feeling of unease she lived with constantly now, had started with the appearance of Caleb in Anna's life. Ruth had been terribly afraid that Caleb was trying to take advantage of her shy, withdrawn *schweschder*, and it had clouded her judgment. She had behaved terribly because of it, which was something she hadn't realized until after the fact.

Anna and Caleb had weathered the storm of fruitless rumors thrust upon them and were now happily married. They seemed to have forgotten the whole mess completely, or at the very least, to have forgiven everyone and put the ordeal out of her mind.

Ruth, however, was having a difficult time doing the same, and she thought about the way she had behaved almost all of the time. It kept her up at night, wondering what inside of her had made her behave so cruelly. It made her question what kind of person she was, and subsequently, what kind of *fraa* she would be when her time came.

That was another source of worry. One that she had

always believed was already all but decided. She and Jonathan had met when they were very young and had been fast friends ever since. As they grew closer to adulthood, that friendship had developed into something deeper. It was widely assumed that when the time was right, she and Jonathan would begin courting.

Ruth had always assumed the same, but now, as Jonathan drew ever closer to the *Rumspringa* that would take him away from her for a whole year, she found it increasingly difficult to maintain faith in the idea. It was as if her refusal to trust Caleb's love for Anna had somehow robbed her of her faith in the sentiment in general.

"Out, here again, are we?" Jonathan spoke up from behind her, rousing her out of her unhappy, tumultuous thoughts. "Your *mamm* told me that she thought you might be. She said you've been spending a good deal of time out here on your own lately. What I can't understand is why."

His voice was playful, as it almost always was, which was something Ruth had always loved about him. At the moment, however, she wanted none of it. She wanted him to be serious with her for a moment, which she felt he should have known. If this was him trying to do that, she feared what was to become of them when he was gone.

"*Ach,* come on now," he continued when she didn't give him the smile he was looking for. "What's that face? Why do you look so serious lately?"

"Because, Jonathan," she answered, trying her best not to look put out and only partially succeeding. "Every day that passes is another day closer to the one when you'll leave me here all alone. You're leaving Faith's Creek, and once you've gone, it won't be long until you forget all about me."

"*Nee,* Ruth," Jonathan objected with a chuckle as he tried to pull her in closer to him, a gesture she steadfastly resisted. "That couldn't be further from the truth. You'll see. I'm going for my *Rumspringa,* as people do..."

"Not every person does," Ruth cut in, mortified by how close to begging him she was getting and yet seemingly unable to stop herself. "Some people stay, don't they? Some people stay right here in town and don't ever go away at all."

Jonathan was quiet for a moment, and Ruth knew

that she had gone just a little too far. More and more lately, this was a conversation the two of them had, and they were never quite able to reach an understanding on the matter.

Ruth had never considered herself the kind of girl to ask such a thing from someone in the first place. Still, the more looming Jonathan's departure was, the more desperate she became.

"It will go by quickly, Ruth," he finally said after taking a deep, measured breath that was surely designed to help him stay calm. "I'll go and then be right back again before you even have time to miss me. And, in the meantime, you'll have your *familye* to look after you and keep you company."

Ruth thought it must be very easy for the person doing the leaving to talk about how quickly the time would pass, but there was one thing Jonathan said that she found both truth and comfort in. She had her *familye,* and as soon as Jonathan took his leave, she hurried from the porch and started off for Anna's new *haus*.

She found her older *schweschder* kneeling in the gardens, which was something she had never done when she lived at the Sutter *haus*, but something she seemed to enjoy immensely now. When Anna glanced up and saw Ruth coming, she got to her feet happily, a broad, lovely smile on her fair face.

Well, now, this is a lovely surprise," she said, hurrying to meet Ruth on the path and pulling her in for a hug. "Although I must say, you don't appear to have your usual carefree air about you. Is something the matter? Have you come to deliver bad news?"

"*Nee,*" Ruth sighed, linking her arm through Anna's and leading them both up the front steps so that they could take a seat on the porch swing that Anna loved so dearly. "There's *nee* bad news, at least not anything new. I've just come from speaking to Jonathan."

"*Ach,*" Anna murmured gently, giving Ruth's hand a reassuring pat. "So he's still planning to leave on his *Rumspringa* soon, is he?"

"*Jah,* any day now," Ruth answered miserably, her eyes welling with helpless tears. "It terrifies me and makes me dreadfully unhappy just to think about it... and yet I can't help thinking that I've brought those feelings on myself."

"What?" Anna asked, pulling back so that she could get a better look at Ruth's face while wearing a startled expression on her own. "What on earth could make you think that? You're such a *wunderbaar* girl, Ruth, truly."

"But I'm not," Ruth whispered, the tears sliding down her cheeks unchecked. "How can you even think that after what I did? I treated Caleb so horribly and hurt you in the process."

Anna was quiet for several seconds, considering Ruth's words. Far from making Ruth nervous that her *schweschder* might decide she agreed, Ruth was grateful to see that she was taking the conversation seriously. She waited for Anna's answer, her hands folded in her lap, and her head bowed meekly.

"Ruth, you were only trying to protect me," Anna finally said, scooting closer again and placing a reassuring arm around Ruth's shoulders. "And I will never fault you for that. Besides, I think it only brought us closer in the end. Just as I think you, too, will soon know the sort of happiness I now live with every day."

"Are you content, Anna?" Ruth asked imploringly,

searching her *schweschder's* kind eyes as she asked her question. "Is this the life you dreamed of?"

"*Ach, nee,*" Anna said, her eyes shining as she shook her eyes. "It's much, much better than anything I could have dreamed up. I can tell you without a single doubt in my heart that I have never before felt more love and understanding than I do with Caleb. There's nobody else in the world I would rather build a *familye* with."

Ruth nodded along to Anna's words, glad to hear that her *schweschder* was so happy. When she saw the way that Anna's hand dropped down to rest protectively on her belly, though, Ruth's eyes widened. Apparently, there was nothing abstract about the comment today.

"Anna!" she exclaimed, her hands flying to her face in surprise. "Are you...?"

"*Jah,*" Anna answered happily before the question was even all of the way out into the world. "We're going to have a *boppli.* So, you see? We can worry and plan all we like, but *Gott* knows what's best for us, and He will lead us down the right path. Just look where He's led me."

Ruth nodded and was relieved to feel the first bit of peace she'd had in days. Perhaps Anna, who had always been the more rational and down to earth of the two, was right.

If Anna and Caleb had been able to overcome such a rocky start to find such happiness, there was *nee* reason to think that Ruth and Jonathan couldn't do the same. After all, they were *not* mere strangers to each other, nor could it be said that they were acquaintances alone. They had already built a foundation for their relationship to stand upon, and she would simply have to trust in it and in *Gott* until Jonathan returned to Faith's Creek.

Grow into Love will be out soon, to find out when join my newsletter

Find all Sarah's books on Amazon and click the yellow follow button

This book is dedicated to the wonderful Amish people and the faithful life that they live.

Go in peace my friends.

As an independent author, Sarah relies on your support. If you enjoyed this book, please leave a review on Amazon or Goodreads.

ABOUT THE AUTHOR

Sarah Miller was born in Pennsylvania and spent her childhood close to the Amish people. Weekends were spent doing chores; quilting or eventually babysitting in the community. She grew up to love their culture and the simple lifestyle and had many Amish friends. The one thing that you can guarantee when you are near the Amish, Sarah believes is that you will feel close to God.

Many years later she married Martin who is the love of her life and moved to England. There she started to write stories about the Amish. Recently after a lot of persuasion from her best friend she has decided to publish her stories. They draw on inspiration from her relationship with the Amish and with God and she hopes you enjoy reading them as much as she did writing them. Many of the stories are based on true events but names have been changed and even though they are authentic at times artistic license has been used.

Sarah likes her stories simple and to hold a message and they help bring her closer to her faith. She currently lives in Yorkshire, England with her husband Martin and seven very spoiled chickens.

She would love to meet you on facebook at https://www.facebook.com/SarahMillerBooks

Sarah hopes her stories will both entertain and inspire and she wishes that you go with God.

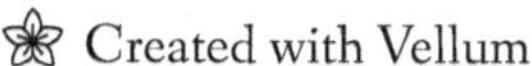 Created with Vellum